World of Insects

Butterflies

by Deirdre A. Prischmann

Consultant:
Gary A. Dunn, MS, Director of Education
Young Entomologists' Society, Inc.
Minibeast Zooseum and Education Center
Lansing, Michigan

Capstone
press
Mankato, Minnesota

Bridgestone Books are published by Capstone Press,
151 Good Counsel Drive, P.O. Box 669, Mankato, Minnesota 56002.
www.capstonepress.com

Library of Congress Cataloging-in-Publication Data
Prischmann, Deirdre A.
    Butterflies / by Deirdre A. Prischmann.
    p. cm.—(Bridgestone Books. World of insects)
    Summary: "A brief introduction to butterflies, discussing their characteristics, habitat, life cycle,
and predators. Includes a range map, life cycle illustration, and amazing facts"—Provided by publisher.
    Includes bibliographical references and index.
    ISBN 0-7368-4335-3 (hardcover)
    1. Butterflies—Juvenile literature. I. Title. II. Series: World of insects.
QL544.2.P75 2006
595.78'9—dc22   2004028517

Editorial Credits
Shari Joffe, editor; Jennifer Bergstrom, set designer; Biner Design, book designer;
    Patricia Rasch, illustrator; Jo Miller, photo researcher; Scott Thoms, photo editor

Photo Credits
Art Directors/John & Jacqueline Wood, 12
Bill Beatty, 10, 18
Bruce Coleman Inc./Fritz Polking, cover; Gail Shumway, 4
Corel, 1
Dwight R. Kuhn, 16
Pete Carmichael, 6
Peter Arnold, Inc./Francois Gilson, 20

1 2 3 4 5 6 10 09 08 07 06 05

Table of Contents

Butterflies

A butterfly flutters by. How can it be so colorful? Its wings are covered with thousands of tiny scales. Together, the scales create many colors and patterns.

Butterflies are insects. All insects have six legs, three body parts, and an **exoskeleton**. The exoskeleton protects the insect's body.

Butterflies and moths are closely related. Butterflies are usually more colorful than moths. Most butterflies fly during the day. Most moths fly at night.

◄ The colors of a butterfly's wings are formed by thousands of tiny scales.

What Butterflies Look Like

Butterflies have long bodies. Their bodies are made up of three parts. The butterfly's head is one part. It holds the eyes, mouthparts, and **antennae**. Butterfly antennae are thin with knobbed ends. Butterflies use their antennae to smell and hear.

The other two parts are the **thorax** and **abdomen**. The thorax is the butterfly's middle section. Four large, flat wings attach to the thorax. The end section is the abdomen. It holds the stomach and heart-like pump.

◀ A butterfly curls up its mouthpart when it's not eating.

Butterfly Range Map

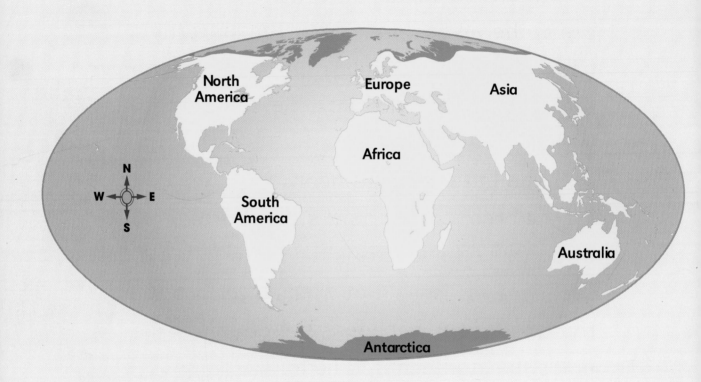

☐ Where Butterflies Live

Butterflies in the World

   More than 17,000 kinds of butterflies
live in the world. Most live in warm, moist
areas. But butterflies can even live in
very dry places if there are flowering
plants around.

   Some butterflies live in cold places.
Mount Everest is home to Apollo butterflies.
Other butterflies live in Siberia. Butterflies
can't live where the weather is too cold.
They can't live at the North or South poles.

Butterfly Habitats

Butterflies live where there are flowering plants. These habitats include grasslands, forests, and wetlands.

Most butterfly caterpillars, or **larvae**, live on the plants they eat. Some kinds of caterpillars live only on certain plants. Female butterflies lay their eggs only on these plants. When the caterpillars hatch, they are already on the kind of plant they eat.

◀ Butterflies sometimes blend in with their surroundings.

What Butterflies Eat

Caterpillars chew up and eat plant leaves. Some caterpillars eat many kinds of plants. Others eat only a few kinds of plants or one kind of plant.

Most adult butterflies feed on sweet nectar from flowers. They suck up nectar with a hollow mouthpart. Butterflies roll up their mouthparts when they aren't feeding.

◄ Caterpillars spend almost all of their time eating.

The Life Cycle of a Butterfly

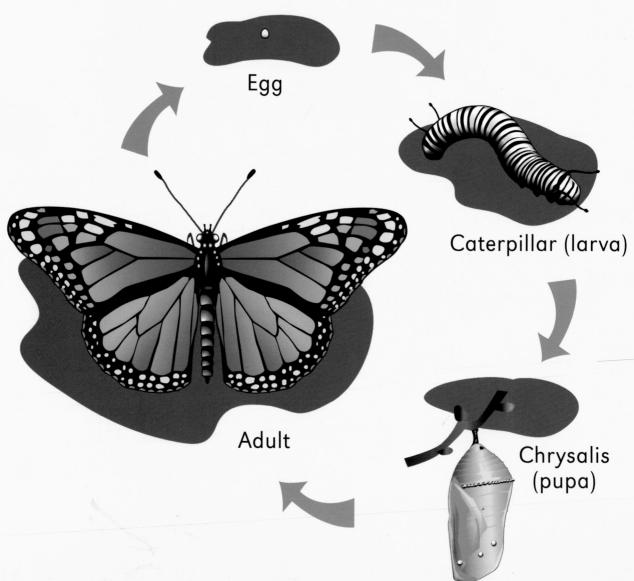

Egg

Caterpillar (larva)

Chrysalis (pupa)

Adult

Eggs and Larvae

Female butterflies mate with males and then lay eggs. A female butterfly lays between 50 and 1,000 eggs. Each egg is about the size of a pinhead. Most eggs hatch in 3 to 10 days.

Caterpillars hatch from the eggs. As they grow, caterpillars **molt**, or shed their exoskeleton, four or five times.

Pupae and Adults

When a caterpillar is about 15 to 30 days old, it stops eating. It attaches itself to a plant. Then it molts one last time and changes into a **pupa**. A butterfly pupa is also called a **chrysalis**. A hard outer shell surrounds the chrysalis.

Inside the chrysalis, the caterpillar slowly changes into a butterfly. After 4 to 14 days, an adult pushes its way out. It rests and opens its wings. As adults, most butterflies live for only a few days or weeks.

◄ After a caterpillar becomes a chrysalis, it slowly changes into an adult butterfly.

Dangers to Butterflies

Butterflies have many predators. Birds, lizards, and spiders eat butterflies and caterpillars. Many butterflies fool predators by blending into their surroundings. Some caterpillars look like bird droppings. Others have sharp spines on their bodies to scare predators.

Some butterflies are in danger. People are destroying their habitats. Many groups are working to protect butterflies. Researchers want these beautiful insects to always have a place on earth.

◀ A spider catches a butterfly in its web.

Amazing Facts about Butterflies

- The largest butterfly is the Queen Alexandra's birdwing. It has a wingspan of 11 inches (28 centimeters).
- Butterflies know right away when they have landed on a sweet flower. That's because they taste with their feet.
- In North America, Monarch butterflies fly south for the winter. They may travel more than 1,500 miles (2,414 kilometers) to their winter homes.

◄ The Queen Alexandra's birdwing butterfly is as big as a bird.

Glossary

abdomen (AB-duh-muhn)—the end section of an insect's body

antenna (an-TEN-uh)—a feeler on an insect's head; more than one antenna are antennae.

chrysalis (KRISS-uh-liss)—a butterfly at the stage of development between a caterpillar and an adult, also called a pupa

exoskeleton (eks-oh-SKEL-uh-tuhn)—the hard outer covering of an insect

larva (LAR-vuh)—an insect at the stage after an egg, also called a caterpillar; more than one larva are larvae.

molt (MOHLT)—to shed an outer layer of skin, or exoskeleton, so a new exoskeleton can be seen

pupa (PYOO-puh)—an insect at the stage of development between a larva and an adult; more than one pupa are pupae.

thorax (THOR-aks)—the middle section of an insect's body; wings and legs are attached to the thorax.

Read More

Llewellyn, Claire. *Butterfly.* Starting Life. Chanhassen, Minn.: NorthWord Press, 2003.

Noonan, Diana. *The Butterfly.* Life Cycles. Philadelphia: Chelsea Clubhouse, 2003.

Internet Sites

FactHound offers a safe, fun way to find Internet sites related to this book. All of the sites on FactHound have been researched by our staff.

Here's how:
1. Visit *www.facthound.com*
2. Type in this special code **0736843353** for age-appropriate sites. Or enter a search word related to this book for a more general search.
3. Click on the **Fetch It** button.

FactHound will fetch the best sites for you!

Index

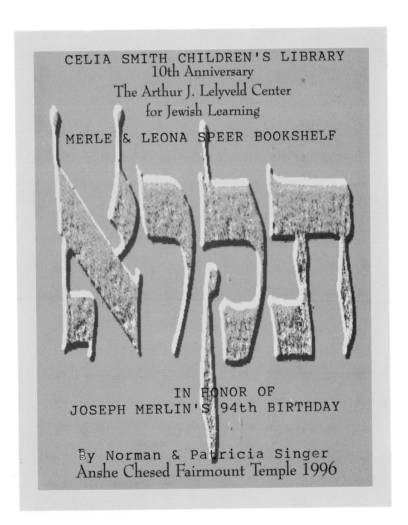

CELIA SMITH CHILDREN'S LIBRARY
10th Anniversary
The Arthur J. Lelyveld Center
for Jewish Learning

MERLE & LEONA SPEER BOOKSHELF

הקריא

IN HONOR OF
JOSEPH MERLIN'S 94th BIRTHDAY

By Norman & Patricia Singer
Anshe Chesed Fairmount Temple 1996

Bim and Bom lived on opposite ends of town.

All week long they were busy working and they didn't get to see each other as much as they would have liked.

But on Shabbat, they could
spend all day together.
So each week they could
hardly wait until it was
Shabbat again.

Bim was a housebuilder, and she built the most wonderful houses in the whole town. She was busy all week building a new house for the mayor, or the grocer, or the rabbi. All day long she would hammer and hammer.

But Friday was different. Every Friday, Bim stopped working on the house she was building.

She knew that some people were too poor to pay her to build them a house, so she spent Fridays building nice, comfortable houses for people who couldn't afford to pay. By the time Shabbat came, she felt she had done something good, done a mitzvah for someone.

Bim loved building, but Bom couldn't even build a birdhouse. Everytime he tried to build something, he would hit his thumb with the hammer.

But Bom loved to bake, and he was the best baker in the whole town. Everyone loved his bread and rolls and muffins.

He was busy all week, baking bread for the teacher, and the artist, and the gardener.

All day long he would knead dough for bread.

But Friday was different. Every Friday, Bom stopped working on the breads he made during the week. On Friday he baked only challah...lots and lots of challah.

He made the most beautiful challah that anyone had ever seen. It was light and sweet, with fancy braids and golden raisins.

On Friday when Bom's challah was baking the whole town smelled wonderful.

Bom knew that not everyone had enough money to buy challah for Shabbat, so he always made extra loaves and gave them to people who could not afford to pay. By the time Shabbat came he felt he had done something good, done a mitzvah.

All Friday long, while Bim was building mitzvah houses, she would look out of the window to watch for the sun to set.

All Friday long, while Bom was baking mitzvah challah, he would listen to the clock in the bakery tick away... one hour, then another, and another.

When it was almost time to light the candles, Bim would put away her tools, wash her hands, brush her hair, and start running to Bom's end of town.

Bom would take off his apron and baker's hat, comb the flour out of his hair, and put a sign on his bakery window: *Closed for Shabbat.* He would start running to Bim's end of town.

They would run and run, until at just the same moment,

they would come to the square in the exact center of town.

Bom would shout out, "Bim!"

Bim would shout out, "Bom!"

They would run to each other, hug, and say,

Shabbat

Shalom

Then they would go off to Bim's
nice, comfortable house, with
Bom's delicious challah, to
celebrate Shabbat together.